Two Women in a Birth

Collection Essential Poets 58

Daphne Marlatt
Betsy Warland

Two Women
in a Birth

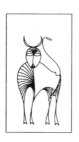

Guernica
Toronto / Montreal / New York
1994

Touch to My Tongue was first published in 1984 by Longspoon Press,
© Daphne Marlatt. *Open Is Broken* was first published in 1984 by Longspoon
Press, © Betsy Warland. *Double Negative* was first published in 1988 by Gynergy Books, © Daphne Marlatt and Betsy Warland. *Reading and Writing
between the Lines* was first published in 1988 in *Tessera* 5. © Daphne Marlatt
and Betsy Warland. *Subject to Change* was first published in 1991 in *The Capilano Review* II, 6/7 and *Trivia* 18, © Daphne Marlatt and Betsy Warland.

Antonio D'Alfonso, Editor
Guernica Editions
P.O. Box 117, Station P, Toronto (Ontario), Canada M5S 2S6
P.O. Box 633, Station N.D.G., Montreal (Quebec), Canada H4A 3R1
340 Nagel Drive, Cheektowaga, N.Y. 14225-4731, USA

Cover design and typesetting by Jean Yves Collette.
Printed in Canada.

Legal Deposit – Second Quarter
National Library of Canada
and Bibliothèque Nationale du Québec.

Canadian Cataloguing in Publication

Marlatt, Daphne, 1942-
Two women in a birth

(Essential poets ; 58)
ISBN 1-55071-003-6

I . Warland, Betsy, 1946- . II . Title.   III . Series.
PS8576 . A74T96 1994   C811 ' . 54   C93-090549-0
PR9199 . 3 . M37T96 1994

Table of Contents

I

DAPHNE MARLATT

TOUCH TO MY TONGUE

For Betsy

*The brain and the womb are both
centres of consciousness, equally
important.*

H.D.
Thought and Vision

*Une femme inscrite en exterritorialité
du langage. Elle expose le sujet comme
on s'expose à la mort. Car il est
question qu'elle vive.*

LOUISE COTNOIR
'S'écrire avec, dans et contre le langage'

This place full of contradiction

a confusion of times if not of place, though you understood
when i said no not the Danish Tearoom – the Indonesian
or Indian, was in fact that place of warm walls, a comfort-
able tarot deck even the lamps pick up your glow, a cabin
of going, fjords in there, a clear and pristine look the winds
weave through your eyes i'm watching you talk of a
different birth, blonde hair on my tongue, of numbers,
nine aflush with capuccino and brandy and rain outside on
that street we flash down, laughing with no umbrella, i see
your face because i don't see mine equally flush with being,
co-incidence being together we meet in these far places we
find in each other, it's Sappho i said, on the radio, always
we meet original, blind of direction, astonished your hand
covers mine walking lowtide strands of Colaba, the light-
house, Mumbai meaning great mother, you wearing your
irish drover's cap and waiting alive in the glow while i come
up worrying danish and curry, this place full of contradic-
tion – you know, you knew, it was the one place i meant.

Houseless

i'm afraid, you say, are you? out in the wintry air, the watery
sun welling close behind your shoulders i am following,
the already known symmetry of your body, its radiant,
bow-woman arched over me, integrity straight as an
arrow. blind with joy i say oh no, thinking, how could i
fear with you?

and now it's dark in here, deep, my cave a house, you on
the other side of the country, our country of sea with the
wind blowing, our country of reeds and grasses under
unfathomed sky. i huddle small, i call you up, a tiny point
of light, memory small like a far-off hole – are you there?
in all this smoke, fear, images torn from the wall requiring
life for a life / that she take it all, mother of giving turned
terrible mother, blood-sipper, sorrow Durga. turning her
back, she takes back what she gives, as you might, or i
might. giving myself up to fear. turning away (for 'safety's'
sake).

there are no walls. fear / love, this light that flashes over the
sea surrounding us. signals danger, yes, my house no
house. i can only be, no vessel but a movement running,
out in the open, out in the dark and rising tide, in risk,
knowing who i am with you –

creatures of ecstasy, we have risen drenched from our own
wet grasses, reeds, sea. turned out, turned inside out, beside
ourselves, we are the tide swelling, we are the continent
draining, deep and forever into each other.

Yes

JADE a sign on the road announces, *ijada, piedra de,* stone of that space between the last rib and the hipbone, that place i couldn't bear the weight of his sleeping hand upon – and my fingers flutter to my ring, gone. only a white band the skin of years hidden under its reminder to my-self of the self i was marrying – 'worthless woman, wilful girl.' Standing athwart, objecting. 'so as to thwart or obstruct', 'perversely'. no, so as to retain this small open space that was mine.

perverse in that, having to defend myself from attack, encroachment on that soft abyss, that tidal place i knew as mine, know now is the place i find with you. not perverse but turned the *right* way round, redefined, it signals us beyond limits in a new tongue our connection runs along. you call me on the phone, have you lost something? and i startle yes. half of it is here, you say. not lost, not lost. broken open on my finger, broken open by your touch, and i didn't even feel a loss, leaving the need for limits at your place, leaving the urge to stand apart i sink into our mouth's hot estuary, tidal yes we are, leaking love and saying it deep within.

Coming to you

through traffic, honking and off-course, direction veering presently up your street, car slam, soon enough on my feet, eager and hesitant, peering with the rush of coming to you, late, through hydrangeas nodding out with season's age, and roses open outline still the edge of summer gone in grounding rain. elsewhere, or from it, i brush by, impatient, bending to your window to surprise you in that place i never know, you alone with yourself there, one leg on your knee, you with boots, with headphones on, grave, rapt with inaudible music. the day surrounds you: point where everything listens. and i slow down, learning how to enter – implicate and unspoken (still) heart-of-the-world.

Kore

no one wears yellow like you excessive and radiant store-
house of sun, skin smooth as fruit but thin, leaking light.
(i am climbing toward you out of the hidden.) no one
shines like you, so that even your lashes flicker light, amber
over blue (*amba,* amorous Demeter, you with the fire in
your hand, i am coming to you). no one my tongue
burrows in, whose wild flesh opens wet, tongue seeks its
nest, amative and nurturing (here i am you) lips work
towards undoing (*dhei,* female, sucking and suckling,
fecund) spurt / spirit opening in the dark of earth, *yu!*
cry jubilant excess, your fruiting body bloom we issue
into the light of, sweet, successive flesh. . .

Eating

a kiwi at four a.m. among the sheets green slice of cool
going down easy on the tongue extended with desire for
you and you in me it isn't us we suck those other lips ton-
gue flesh wet wall that gives and gives whole fountains
inner mountains moving out resistances you said ladders
at the canyon leap desire is its way through walls swerve
fingers instinct in you insist further persist in me too wave
on wave to that deep pool we find ourselves / it dawning on
us we have reached the same place 'timeless' you recognize
as 'yes' giving yourself not up not in we come suddenly
round the bend to it descending with the yellow canyon
flow the mouth everything drops away from time its sheets
two spoons two caved-in shells of kiwi fruit

Climbing the canyon even as

the Fraser rushes out to sea and you, where you are i am,
muddy with heartland silt beside the river's outward push
my car climbs steadily away from and toward – where we
were – each step we took, what you said, what i saw (sun in
your hair on the rim of your look), smell of love on our skin
as we rushed with the river's push out, out to the mouth
taking everything with us / and away, as i leave you there
(where i am still) to make this climb i don't want to, feel
how it hurts, our pull, womb to womb, spun thin reaching
Sailor's Bar, Boston Bar, reaching Lytton where the
Thompson River joins, alone nosing my way into the
unnamed female folds of hill, soft sage since we came down
twelve days ago begun to bloom, gold and the grass gold,
and your hair not gold but like as light shivers through these
hills. i am waiting for the dark, waiting with us at Ashcroft,
behind glass, by the river's edge: then going down to it, that
bank of uncertain footing as the freight roars by, across, that
black river in its rush, noisy, enveloping us as we envelop
each other – and the wind took your hair and flung it
around your look, exultant, wild, i felt the river pushing
through, all that weight of heartlocked years let loose and
pouring with us out where known ground drops away and
i am going, beyond the mountains, past the Great Divide
where rivers run in opposite direction i am carrying you
with me.

Prairie

in this land the rivers carve furrows and canyons as sudden
to the eye as if earth opened up its miles and miles of roll-
ing range, highway running to its evercoming horizon,
days of it, light picking flowers. your blackeyed susans are
here, my coral weed in brilliant patches, and always that
grass frayed feathery by the season, late, and wild canada
geese in the last field. i imagine your blue eye gathering
these as we go, only you are not here and the parched flat
opens up: badlands and hoodoos and that river with
dangerous currents you cannot swim, TREACHEROUS BANK,
sandstone caving in: and there she goes, Persephone caught
in a whirlwind the underside churns up, the otherwise of
where we are, cruising earth's surface, gazing on it, grazing,
like those 70 million year old dinosaurs, the whole herd
browsing the shore of Bearpaw Sea which ran all the way
in up here, like Florida, she said, come in from the desert
region they were hungry for grass (or flowers) when some-
thing like a flashflood caught them, their bones, all these
years later, laid out in a whirlpool formation i cannot see
(that as the metaphor) up there on the farthest hoodoo,
those bright colours she keeps stressing, the guy in the red
shirt, metal flashing, is not Hades but only the latest tech-
nician in a long line of measurers. and earth? i have seen her
open up to let love in, let loose a flood, and fold again, so
that even my fingers could not find their way through all
that bush, all that common day rolling unbroken.

Hidden ground

lost without you, though sun accompanies me, though moon and the maps say always i am on the right track, the Trans-Canada heading east – everything in me longs to turn around, go back to you, to (that gap), afraid i'm lost, afraid i've driven out of our territory we found (we inhabit together), not *terra firma,* not dry land, owned, along the highway, cleared for use, but that other, low-lying, moist and undefined, hidden ground, wild and running everywhere along the outer edges. lost, *losti,* lust-y one, who calls my untamed answering one to sally forth, finding alternate names, finding the child provoked, invoked, lost daughter, other mother and lover, waxing tree, waist i love, water author sounding the dark edge of the word we come to, augur-ess, *issa,* lithesome, *lilaiesthai,* yearning for you, and like a branch some hidden spring pulls toward our ground, i grow unafraid increasing ('lust of the earth or of the plant'), *lasati,* (she) yearns and plays, letting the yearning play it out, playing it over, every haystack, every passing hill, that tongue our bodies utter, woman tongue, speaking in and of and for each other.

Where we went

we went to what houses stars at the sea's edge, brilliant day, where a metal crab jets water catching light, heaven and earth in a tropic embrace joined upright, outside glass doors people and cars and waterglaze. city that houses stares, city that houses eyes, electricity writing the dark of so many heads figuring where we were. we knew so well i didn't even catch your eye as we stepped through and she brought out the rings for us to look at, silver, moon metal inscribed in the shape of wild eyes by kwagiul and haida hands, raven and wolf and whale and unknown birds not seen in the light city. creatures of unorganized territory we become, a *physical impulse* moving from me to you (the poem is), us *dancing in animal skins* in the unmapped part of our world. now you wear whale on the finger that enters and traces in whale walrus the horse you thought i was, shy of fences, running the edge of the woods where brought up short i feel the warmth of you, double you, wolf. i wear wolf and dream of your lean breast descending, warm and slow the fur that grows between your eyes fifteen hundred miles away in another city under the same moon.

Down the season's avenue

sunrise 7:18, sunset 7:23: we are approaching that point when the pivot of dawn and the pivot of night balance the narrowing day. you in it far off on the coast climbing what tree over the sea to gaze east? everywhere i see light lean along a curved plain. no intimate clefts of earth, no hilly rise but plain ('flat, clear') under the eye of horizon, that boundary you are on the other side of, two hours earlier. flat, *plano-* plain as the palm of my hand, but i can't see. i try the trees for company, these lives, leaves, sudden against their going, lucid and startled. i ride their coming into view, not knowing, whispering where are you? down the avenue your breath runs up my spine, you shiver through, clear as the fire in turning leaves, clear as your voice that lights i'm here, clear as that point when the plane comes in and you will be standing there. i'm coming home.

In the dark of the coast

there is fern and frost, a gathering of small birds melting
song in the underbrush. close, you talk to one. there is the
cedar slant of your hair as it falls gold over your shoulder,
over your naked, dearly known skin – its smell, its answering
touch to my tongue. fondant, font, found, all that melts,
pours. the dark rain of our being together at last. and the
cold wind, curled-up fronds of tree fern wanting touch,
our fingers separate and stiff. we haven't mourned enough,
you say, for our parting, lost to each other the last time
through. in the dark of this place, its fire touch, not fern
but frost, just one of the houses we pass through in the
endless constellation of our being, close, and away from
each other, torn and apart. i didn't know your hair, i
didn't know your skin when you beckoned to me in that
last place. but i knew your eyes, blue, as soon as you came
around the small hill, knew your tongue. come, you said,
we slid together in the spring, blue, of a place we'd been.
terra incognita known, *geysa,* gush, upwelling in the hid-
den Norse we found, we feel it thrust as waters part for us,
hot, through fern, frost, volcanic thrust. it's all there, love,
we part each other coming to, geyser, spouting pool,
hidden in and under separate skin we make for each other
through.

Coming up from underground

out of the shadows of your being, so sick and still a shade
under it, your eye looks out at me, grave and light at once,
smiling recognition. draw close, i am so glad to see you,
bleak colour of your iris gone blue, that blue of a clear sky,
belo, bright, Beltane, 'bright-fire'. draw me in, light a new
flame after your sudden descent into the dark. draw me
close so i see only light your eye a full moon rides, *bleikr* in
the old tongue, shining, white, ascent above horizon
fringed with black reed, horsetail, primitive flicker on the
rim of eons ascending this white channel we wander in, a
plain of 'wild beestes' felt at the periphery of vision, fear
and paranoia ready to spring – beyond the mind or out of
it they say, though 'defended. . . with apparent logic'. in
this landscape we are undefended in the white path of
our being, lunar and pulled beyond reason. *bleikr,* shining
white, radiant healing in various bright colours, *blanda,*
to mingle and blend: the blaze of light we are, spiralling.

Healing

stray white lips, petals kissing middle distance between
blue iris you, me, moss there and small starred dandelions.
in the drift gathering, days, hours without touch. gauze,
waiting for the two lips of your incision to knit, waiting
for our mouths to close lip to other lip in the full spring of
wet, revived, season plants come alive. this season of your
body traumatized, muscles torn where the knife went, a
small part of you gone. gall, all that is bitter, melancholy.

each day we climb a small hill, looking. rufous humm-
ingbirds dive before our very eyes kissing space. fawn lilies
spring moist lips to wing filled air. i want to open you like
a butterfly. over bluffs the rim of blue distance we might
leap, free fall, high above us four bald eagles scream for
pure glee. glee, it falls on us, bits of sound shining, rain of
rung glass. glisten, glare. (g)listen, all of it goes back
shining, even *gall* does, glass and glazing, every yellow
hope a spark, lucid and articulate in the dark i wake to,
reaching for you. somewhere a bird calls. it is our bird, the
one that wings brightness, *springan,* scattering through us
as your lips open under mine and the new rain comes at
last, lust, springs in us beginning all over again.

Notes

This place full of contradiction

Mumbai is the vernacular name for Bombay, after the Koli goddess Mumbai (derived from Maha Amba, Great Mother). According to L.F. Rushbrook Williams in *A Handbook for Travellers in India, Pakistan, Nepal, Bangladesh and Sri Lanka,* she is the tutelary deity of this island, once seven islands separated at high tide, drained and reclaimed by the British. The southernmost tip is the site of the Colaba lighthouse.

Houseless

Durga, or Kali, 'the "Unapproachable" and "Perilous" ', is the deadly aspect of the goddess who is also World Mother (Jagad-Amba). See Erich Neumann, *The Great Mother,* p. 151-2.

Yes

piedra de ijada or stone of the flank is the Spanish name for jade, once believed to be a cure for kidney disease. 'Jade' has also been used (by men) as a denigratory term for a woman.

Kore

the story of Persephone's abduction by Hades and her subsequent reunion with Demeter is uniquely the story of the relationship between daughter (kore, maiden) and mother (De-meter, earth mother). It forms the heart of the rituals celebrated at Eleusis. 'It was her own daughter who was buried under earth, and yet the core of *herself* died with her and came back to life only when Persephone – flower sprout, grain sprout – rose again from the earth.' Nor Hall, *The Moon and the Virgin,* p. 83. 'Every woman's womb, the mortal image of the earth mother, Demeter. . .' J.J. Bachofen, *Myth, Religion, and Mother Right,* p. 80.

dhei is the Indo-European root of 'female' and means 'to suckle' but has diversified into *fetus* (offspring, that which sucks), *fellatio* (sucking) and *felix* (fruitful, happy).

yu is the Indo-European root of 'you', second person pronoun; also an outcry as in Latin *jubilare,* 'to raise a shout of joy' (as the initiates at Eleusis might have done on seeing the luminous form of the risen Kore).

Hidden ground

affiliate words for 'lust' are Old Norse *losti* (sexual desire), Gothic *lustus* (desire), Greek *lilaiesthai* (to yearn), Sanskrit *lasati* (he yearns, he plays).

-*ess* is of course the English suffix indicating the female, derived from Latin *issa*.

Where we went

the poet Alexandra Grilikhes, in an article entitled 'Dancing in Animal Skins', speaks of reading poetry to an audience as a shamanic act: 'the poet dances in animal skins to evoke in you what longs to be evoked or released'; 'the speaking of poetry is above all a physical impulse, and the performance of the poem *is* the poem.'

Coming up from underground

'bleak' derives from Old Norse *bleikja,* white colour, rooted in Indo-European *bhel-* with its powerful cluster of meanings and associations: to shine, flash, burn, shining white and various bright colours, fire; *belo-,* bright, Beltane (the Celtic May Day festival celebrated with bonfires burning on the hills), Old Norse *bleikr,* shining, white, and *blanda,* to mingle and blend.

Healing

the etymology of 'gall' as in gallstone is interesting; it goes back to Indo-European *ghel-,* to shine, spawning words for colours, bright materials and bile or gall in a range from Germanic *gelwaz* (yellow) to Greek *khole* (bile, from which we get melancholy) to Germanic *gladaz* (from which we get glad), *glasam* (glass, glaze), Middle Dutch *glisteren* (shine), Old English *glēo* (glee).

Musing with mothertongue

the beginning: language, a living body we enter at birth, sustains and contains us. it does not stand in place of anything else, it does not replace the bodies around us. placental, our flat land, our sea, it is both place (where we are situated) and body (that contains us), that body of language we speak, our mothertongue. it bears us as we are born in it, into cognition.

language is first of all for us a body of sound. leaving the water of the mother's womb with its dominant sound, we are born into this other body whose multiple sounds bathe our ears from the moment of our arrival. we learn the sounds before we learn what they say: a child will speak baby-talk in pitch patterns that accurately imitate the sentence patterns of her mothertongue. an adult who cannot read or write will speak his mothertongue without being able to say what a particular morpheme or even word in a phrase means. we learn nursery rhymes without understanding what they refer to. we repeat skipping songs significant for their rhythms. gradually we learn how the sounds of our language are active as meaning and then we go on learning for the rest of our lives what the words are actually saying.

in poetry, which has evolved out of chant and song, in riming and tone-leading, whether they occur in prose or poetry, sound will initiate thought by a process of association. words call each other up, evoke each other, provoke each other, nudge each other into utterance. we know from dreams and schizophrenic speech how deeply association works in our psyches, a form of thought that is not rational but erotic because it works by attraction. a drawing, a pulling toward. a 'liking'. Germanic *līk-*, body, form; like, same.

like the atomic particles of our bodies, phonemes and syllables gravitate toward each other. they attract each other in movements we call assonance, euphony, alliteration, rhyme. they are drawn together and echo each other in rhythms we identify as feet – lines run on, phrases patter like speaking feet. on a macroscopic level, words evoke each other in movements we know as puns and figures of speech (these endless similes, this continuing fascination with making one out of two, a new one, a simultitude.) meaning moves us deepest the more of the whole field it puts together, and so we get sense where it borders on nonsense ('what is the sense of it all?') as what we sense our way into. the sentence. ('life.') making our multiplicity whole and even intelligible by the end-point. intelligible: logos there in the gathering hand, the reading eye.

hidden in the etymology and usage of so much of our vocabulary for verbal communication (contact, sharing) is a link with the body's physicality: matter (the import of what you say) and matter and by extension mother; language and tongue; to utter and outer (give birth again); a part of speech and a part of the body; pregnant with meaning; to mouth (speak) and the mouth with which we also eat and make love; sense (meaning) and that with which we sense the world; to relate (a story) and to relate to somebody, related (carried back) with its connection with bearing (a child); intimate and to intimate; vulva and voluble; even sentence which comes from a verb meaning to feel.

like the mother's body, language is larger than us and carries us along with it. it bears us, it births us, insofar as we bear with it. if we are poets we spend our lives discovering not just what *we* have to say but what language is saying as it carries us with it. in etymology we discover a history of verbal relations (a family tree, if you will) that has preceded us and given us the world we live in. the given, the immediately presented, as at birth – a given name a given world. we know language structures our world and in a crucial sense we cannot see what we cannot verbalize, as the work of Whorf and ethnolinguistics has pointed out to us. here we are truly contained within the body of our mothertongue. and even the physicists, chafing at these limits, say that the glimpse physics now gives us of the nature of the universe cannot be conveyed in a language based on the absolute difference between a noun and a verb. poetry has been demonstrating this for some time.

if we are women poets, writers, speakers, we also take issue with the given, hearing the discrepancy between what our patriarchally-loaded language bears (can bear) of our experience and the difference from it our experience bears out – how it misrepresents, even miscarries, and so leaves unsaid what we actually experience. can a pregnant woman be said to be 'master' of the gestation process she finds herself within – is that her relationship to it? (see Julia Kristeva, *Desire in Language,* p. 238.) are women included in the statement 'God appearing as man' (has God ever appeared as a woman?) can a woman ever say she is 'lady of all she surveys' or could others ever say of her she 'ladies it over them'?

so many terms for dominance in English are tied up with male experiencing, masculine hierarchies and differences (exclusion), patriarchal holdings with their legalities. where are the poems that celebrate the soft letting-go the flow of menstrual blood is as it leaves her body? how can the standard sentence structure of English with its linear authority, subject through verb to object, convey the wisdom of endlessly repeating and not exactly repeated cycles her body knows? or the mutuality her body shares embracing other bodies, children, friends, animals, all those she customarily holds and is held by? how can the separate nouns mother and child convey the fusion, bleeding womb-infant mouth, she experiences in those first days of feeding? what syntax can carry the turning herself inside out in love when she is both sucking mouth and hot gush on her lover's tongue?

Julia Kristeva says: 'If it is true every national language has its own dream language and unconscious, then each of the sexes – a division so much more archaic and fundamental than the one into languages – would have its own unconscious wherein the biological and social program of the species would be ciphered in confrontation with language, exposed to its influence, but independent from it' (*Desire in Language,* p. 241). i link this with the call so many feminist writers in Quebec have issued for a language that returns us to the body, a woman's body and the largely unverbalized, presyntactic, postlexical field it knows. postlexical in that, as Mary Daly shows, with intelligence (that gathering hand) certain words (dandelion sparks) seed themselves back to original and originally-related meaning. this is a field where words mutually attract each other, fused by connection, enthused (inspired) into variation (puns, word play, rime at all levels) fertile in proliferation (offspring, rooting back to *al-,* seed syllable to grow, and leafing forward into *alma,* nourishing, a woman's given name, soul, inhabitant.)

inhabitant of language, not master, not even mistress, this new woman writer (Alma, say) in having is had, is held by it, what she is given to say. in giving it away is given herself, on that double edge where she has always lived, between the already spoken and the unspeakable, sense and nonsense. only now she writes it, risking nonsense, chaotic language leafings, unspeakable breaches of usage, intuitive leaps. inside language she leaps for joy, shoving out the walls of taboo and propriety, kicking syntax, discovering life in old roots.

language thus speaking (i.e. inhabited) relates us, 'takes us back' to where we are, as it relates us to the world in a living body of verbal relations. articulation: seeing the connections (and the thighbone, and the hipbone, etc.). putting the living body of language together means putting the world together, the world we live in: an act of composition, an act of birthing, us, uttered and outered there in it.

II

BETSY WARLAND

OPEN IS BROKEN

For Daphne

Untying the tongue

what prompted me to write *open is broken* was the realization that the English language tongue-ties me. this 'restricted mobility' was most apparent in my attempts to speak of my erotic life. such speechlessness is not peculiar to me. few erotic texts exist in north american women's writing. is it taboo? TABOO: 'ta, mark + bu, exceedingly'. are women afraid to 'mark' the paper? or as Hélène Cixous writes, 'inscribe' ourselves? it is difficult. women already feel (are) far too vulnerable in this society. 'To write: I am a woman is heavy with consequences' (Nicole Brossard, *These Our Mothers*).

'Patriarchal development of consciousness has an indisputable inner need to 'murder the mother', that is, as far as possible to negate, exclude, devalue, and repress the 'maternal-feminine' world which represents the unconscious' (Erich Neumann, 'Narcissism, Normal Self-Formation and the Primary Relation to the Mother').

immediately surfaces the second intimidation: fear of narcissism. though few mirrors stand in which we can see our eroticism reflected, we are terrorized by the thought of this accusation. safer to have no 'marks'. no marks? pornography is ignorance. and romance? we have been per-

TABOO   **ROMANCE**

suaded to believe eroticism in romance. ROMANCE: 'made in Rome'. so much for romance! the word itself connotes fabricating an image *outside* ourselves compared to discovery of the erotic wellspring *within.*

'Where the god is male and father only, and. . . is associated with law, order, civilization, *logos* and super-ego, religion – and the pattern of life which it encourages – tends to become a matter of these only, to the neglect of nature, instinct. . . feeling, *eros,* and what Freud called the 'id'. Such a religion, so far from 'binding together' and integrating, may all too easily become an instrument of repression, and so of individual and social disintegration' (Victor White, *Soul and Psyche: An Enquiry Into the Relationship of Psychotherapy and Religion*).

the language itself does not reflect women's sensual experience. for most of us, however, it is our native tongue. the only language we have. *open is broken* is about the words i abandoned. ABANDON: '(to put) in one's power; a, to, at, from Latin ad, to + bandon, power.' so, when we abandon words, it isn't a simple matter of leaving them behind but rather a turning over of our power *to* those who keep them: speechlessness the consequence.

the word is the act. when i abandon a word i relinquish the experience it calls up. yet, how can i use the word 'intercourse' as a lesbian? and what do i say as a feminist, when

ABANDON   **DISMEMBERED**

in my deepest erotic moments words like 'surrender' pulse in my head? a dictionary defines surrender as: 'to relinquish possession or control of to another because of demand or compulsion.' still, my body insisted, my instincts persisted / pulled me toward this word. it seemed full of life, and indeed, in IX, i find it is. truth is in the roots.

contemporary *usage* of our words is what tongue-tied me. the repressed is the absent. women have been DISMEMBERED: 'dis-, (removal) + membrum, member' from the word. in tracing words back, i have found that etymology often re-members the feminine sensibility of our inner landscapes.

usage is selective. Cixous writes: 'I maintain unequivocally that there is such a thing as *marked* writing; that, until now, far more extensively and repressively than is ever suspected or admitted, writing has been run by a libidinal and cultural – hence political, typically masculine – economy; that this is a locus where the repression of women has been perpetuated. . . that this locus has grossly exaggerated all signs of sexual opposition (and not sexual difference), where woman has never her *turn* to speak' ('Laugh of the Medusa').

Mary Daly describes the dominance of male culture as the 'presence of absence'. this presence of absence in our language has resulted in the abandonment of our most significant words. tongue-tied. no marks. no rituals. RITUAL:

RITUAL   RITE   RETURN   MARK

'rite.' RITE: 'retornāre, to return.' RETURN: 'turn, threshold, thread.' the thread knotted around our tongues – untied, spirals us to the edge. MARK: 'merg-, boundary, border, marking out the boundary by walking around it (ceremonially 'beating the bounds').'

mark of the spirit. painted bodies. marked objects. sacred openings. threshold to altered states. TABOO: 'exceedingly marked, marked as sacred.' invisible made visible.

abandoned words spring up from deep places. claiming our eroticism reclaims the dismembered.

'homesick without memory
yet tongues are not fooled
tissue "clairvoyant"
memorized, re-members "chiaroscuro" history'

(XI)

Audrey Lourde, in her essay 'Uses of the Erotic: the Erotic as Power', names the erotic 'the nurturer or nursemaid of all our deepest knowledge'. tracing the etymology of abandoned words has that same reconstructive power. reclaims what we subconsciously know, passionately BELIEVE: 'leubh-, livelong, love, libido'.

intact. the texts woven in / are the very fibers of our tissue. TISSUE: 'teks-, text'. the body of language whole again.

TABOO   **BELIEVE**   **TISSUE**

Daphne Marlatt, in her poetic statement 'musing with mothertongue', characterizes this phenomenon: 'inhabitant of language, not master, not even mistress, this new woman writer. . . in having is had, is held by it, what she is given to say. in giving it away is given herself, on that double edge where she has always lived, between the already spoken and the unspeakable, sense and non-sense. only now she writes it, risking nonsense, chaotic language leafings, unspeakable breaches of usage, intuitive leaps. inside language she leaps for joy, shoving out the walls of taboo and propriety, kicking syntax, discovering life in old roots.'

writing comes out of chaos much as Eros was born out of Chaos. in trusting the relationship between eroticism / etymology and tissue / text, the language – my language – broke open. my tongue freed. to mark exceedingly.

Induction

showing 'our sexts'

women's texts subtext
between

         the

                     lines

context pretext *text:*
'in the original language, as opposed to a translation
or rendering'

         pre-text

mother tongue: 'a language from which other languages
originate'

tonguetext

      'kissing vulva lips
      tongues torque way into vortext
      leave syllables behind

      sound we are sound
      original vocabulary
      language: "lingua, tongue" '

                  (VI)

      sentence: 'sent, sense, presentiment, scent'

scentext

> 'the pen gets on the scent' (Virginia Woolf)

> > > > > syntax

one long sentence

> 'homesickness without memory
> yet tongues are not fooled
> tissue "clairvoyant" '

> > > (XI)

> > > > *tissue:* 'teks-, to weave,

> text, context, pretext, tela'

> > ***telatext***

> > > *tela:* 'a weblike membrane

> that covers some portion of a bodily organ'

> > > > *hymen:* 'to bind, sew,

seam, suture'

'you opened me. . .
an eye with no mind i stood skinless before you'

> > > (I)

> > > we the weavers and the web

webstertext

> Mary Daly's 'websters'

> > > *webster:* a weaver (Old English

webbestre, feminine of webba, or weaver, from webb,
a web)'

between

> > > the

> > > > > lines

39

the

                warp

                                          is

warp: 'wer-, inward, verse, version, vertigo, vortex, invert, subvert, universe, prose'

vortext

      'then she was pulled into a whirlpool
      claim, surrender, sow, manure flying out
      words her tongue never trusted
      words from another place, old place, vaguely
      remembered'

                                      (VIII)

'Her flesh speaks true' (Hélène Cixous)

                      tissuetext

                            tissue: 'the
substance, structure, or texture of which an animal or plant body, or any organ of it, is composed'

                text the tissue   one long
sentence   no period   we   are   menses   flow
period: 'sed- to go, exodus'

                  are exodus

                        'going around in circles'

                                (IV)

                            exotext

one long embrace

      'texts of our bodies (tongue come)'

                      (X)

                          the route

'the route her tongue took

the route of the word'
                              (VIII)
                                    'root up the word trees
                                    in the manure the manuscript'
                                                      (VII)
                                          tree: 'deru, truth' is

in the roots
        etymotext
                        is in the route
                                                      erostext

'you claim me with your tongue
speak my skin's syntax
know my desire's etymology, idiom'
                        (IX)
intertextuality
                        intersect/uality

                                          intersexuality
'involve,
        revolve,
                evolve,
                        vulva'
                        (X)
                                inhertertuality

Up from under

I

these are the words commonly used to describe our love:
    degenerate
    destructive
    perverted
    unnatural
    narcissistic
    disgusting
    dirty
    obscene
    queer
    repulsive
    self-indulgent
    sick
    evil
evil: 'upo, under, up from under, over, uproar, open'

II

in the year 1982 on the sixth day of the eighth month we
put on the silver curve of each other's presence with rings
of wilderness wolf & whale and committed *exogamy:*

'the custom of marrying outside the tribe, family, clan or
social unit'

outside
not into

        up from under
        uproar
        open

III

        evil ring   open ring
        the snake uncurls

'The world of vision has been symbolized in all ages. . .
in all countries by the serpent'
                        comes
up from under

'a snake in the corner of the map marks where the un-
known begins'

where our home begins

the snake
found round
our fingers

Receiving the seed

she turns toward me
rings me in
holds me fiercely
as a tree its shadow a shadow its tree
intense: 'intendere, to stretch toward'
i want her evident in me
her seed
ring in my ring
i have never desired it before
before was not her
we enter, *inter-*
course: 'intercurrere, to run between'
ring's turning boundary become
vortext (inner course)
her seed in me rolls
end   over   end   falling   tipping   rising
down my clapping tunnel in
                              to glowing orbit
first moon in my galaxy

Crafts(man)ship

i write you:
'the crows are cawing the roses are finished
bouquets i arrange
of flowers remaining
frighten the cats'.

i saw you
in the new anthology
a review copy handed to me
photograph a you of teeth clenched on edge/brink of
your poems' (s)killed sadness
the courage the cowardice of crafts(man)ship

craft: 'strength, skill'
(s)kill(man)ship
skill: 'cutlass, shield, scalp'
read:
'a forceful writer'
'the thrust of his line'

i heard you
years before
in a poem here and there
my tongue familiar with your name
its syllables a tune in my head

this photograph
the mask i met mirror i saw
     my own in
double reflection
a living in parenthesis
recognized, released

'Courage is worthless in itself. . . one must pass
through it'

ship ahoy
ship abandoned

'the dahlia looks in my door open / lifts
its head above ordered green stares
red entire'

as the now of your face unbolted

Open is broken

Prologue

the talisman for their love
a tornado in her hand.
she had found the old woman on the stone
the surrounding maze had not confounded her.
she asked her questions in the flash of time allowed
'should i pursue this love?'

                        'yes.'

'will it be painful?'

                'yes.'

'are we archetypes?'

                'yes'

then it was time for the talisman.

                                'open your right hand.'

a tornado emerged as the fingers unfolded
she shook
yet felt the calm of its eye within / re-membered
the egg
origin of all

            'open is broken.'

pecking her way out
she heard a voice tranquilly say
'consider me dangerous'
recognized it
as her own

I

it is morning
the animals are out early
sniffing and switching their tails
sense something in the garden not present before

i move carefully
an egg without shell, yolk and white shimmering
an eye alone trembling
an image among
images without meaning except in relation

you opened me
whispered 'come back' was it
some other life between us before?

an eye with no mind i stood skinless before you
a flower unbolted, quivering in its moment

the animals are out early
sniffing and switching their tails
sense surrender

as you left
you called 'come see the moon!'
its full eye stared at me
it knows about breaking

II

the roses rise up
stretch into morning
each bush a brothel of red and pink orgy of opening
petals provoke
the do of desire
come womb-wooing
tongues bloom blooming

III

the leaves witness you unsheathing me
my bud my bud quivering in your
mouth you *leaf* me (leaf: 'peel off')
in front of a window full of green eyes we climb
the green *ladder:* 'clitoris, incline, climax'
on the tip of your tongue you flick
me leaf: 'lift' up
to tip tree top
point of all i am to the sky
'roof of the world'
leaves
sink slow into darkening
with my resin on your swollen lips
leave us in our
betrothal: 'truth, tree'

IV

the tree tides out of itself
ring: 'search, circle, crest'
spirals its truth
going around in circles
we ex-changed rings
'Latin ex-, from ex, out, out of'
out of change we wear the sign of search shared
H.D.'s trees, 'concentric circles'
Virginia 'The being grows rings, like a tree'
Nicole's spiralling lines
and your rings of consciousness in '69
you, my lover of endless eyes, of 'rings within rings'

V

'small hill' becomes sun
'incline(s)' in my mouth
smooth burning on my tongue
south in the mouth of north
star radiant
centre of our system
heartbeats a heart hungry
comes come spilling everywhere
leaving no darkness in me no corner of refusal
the light the light words ignite that have nursed their
nightmares
fondled fears inherited
we do not fall off
perspective is a line given us
with your sun
rising is setting
centrifugal: centripetal
we enter our horizons and do not vanish

VI

bodies joined north and south
we are each other's entrance

kissing vulva lips
tongues torque way into vortex
leave syllables behind

sound we are sound
original vocabulary
language: 'lingua, tongue'
not separate but same
this is how we came

we have been here before
we are here before
other times other tongues
uterus the *universe:*
'ūniversus, whole, entire, turned into one'

VII

the k(no)wing is the telling
is the leaving some things out

root up the word trees
in the manure the manuscript

the sows have come home

VIII

when she began she used words like moon, egg
words that did not startle
then she was pulled into a whirlpool
claim, surrender, sow, manure flying out
words her tongue never trusted
words from another place, old place, vaguely remembered

each time they slid between the sheets to open each other
they slid between the pages of an ancient text
                    turns of a hidden scroll
the bed the *map:* 'napkin, sheet, cloth'

the route her tongue took
the root of the word

you claim me with your tongue
speak my skin's syntax
know my desire's etymologies, *idiom:*
'idios, own, personal, separate'
indigenous imagery
no longer indecipherable i *surrender:*

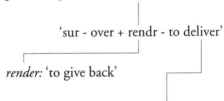

'sur - over + rendr - to deliver'

render: 'to give back'

deliver: 'dē-completely+līberāre-to set free'

the code broken by your fluency
fluent: 'soft, wet, naked, exposed'
you part the covers
                    to set free

urged by your *fluency:* 'to swell, well up, overflow'
our fluids spout out hot gold
                        rivulets punctuating ecstasy

X

egg broken
mouth open
tongues *bloom:* 'blow'
tornados cresting our *mounds:*
'manure, manuscript, command'
texts of our bodies (tongue come)
under the *tornado* 's: 'moan'
surrendering ground hungry for home

XI

the *claim?*
between your legs home soil
homesickness without memory
yet tongues are not fooled
tissue 'clairvoyant'
memorizes, re-members 'chiaroscuro' history
at your taste i 'cry out'
'reclaim(ed)' by the 'Paraclete'

XII

soil: (verb) 'to make dirty, defile, pollute with sin'
from 'pig, hyena, sow'
soil: (verb) 'to siege'
dirty sows. . .
this soil's noun 'filth, stain'
this soil's noun 'manure'
its noun
its name

XIII

soil: (noun) 'top layer of the earth's surface, land, country'
from 'sit, seat'

seat: 'a place in which one may sit
    the buttocks
    residence
    a center of authority'

between your legs
home soil, native soil
land things grow, flourish, thrive in
you re-turn me to the noun
the 'found/ation'

XIV

wer - wel - kwel:
'to turn; to turn; to revolve'

wer; 'verse, version' the k(no)wing is the telling
'invert, universe, vortex, vertigo'
the palimpsest your body

wer - wel - kwel

wel: 'helix, volume, involve, revolve, evolve, vulva' ear
hearing all

wer - wel - kwel

kwel: 'cycle, wheel, talisman'
the talisman for their love
a tornado in her hand

wer - wel - kwel:
'to turn; to turn, to revolve, dwell'

XV

helix: 'a volute on a Corinthian or Ionic capital'
is this when the helix was changed
this when tornado tongues became
'scroll-like ornament'
on virile columns?

helix: 'wellspring' of our hearts
'three-dimensional curve that lies on a cylinder or cone
and cuts the elements at a constant angle'

helix: 'volume(s)' of our obliterated stories
secreted in our bodies
helix: 'the folded rim of skin around the outer ear'
helix: 'involve, revolve, evolve, vulva' ear
hearing all
forgetting nothing

XVI

this is a place we touch and taste each other to
where the *person:* 'persona, mask' falls away

faces forget disguise
when no longer set against uncertainty
re-turn

in your mirrors is the face of one just dead
fear re-formed into lyric

clarity, it is a kind of death
we are claimed
surrender, resist nothing

i kiss you after we pass through
i kiss a cloud

XVII

]
[
]
[
]
[
no words
]
listen
[
wind: of our
]
being
[
'air'
]
'aura'
[
'wing' / each
]
a wing
[
riding
]
our own wind
[
'weather, storm'
]
'wē, wing, to blow'
[
wing / each
]

a wing
[
the body invisible between us
]
'vāti, (s)he blows, Nirvana'
[
the body
]
Nirvana between us
[
]
[

XVIII

as you hold this / these pages throb
a radiant throat in your hands
each line a wave / blood / pulse
beware
words alter *change:*
'to curve, bend'

you expected to be uneasy
(wave / blood / pulse)
but not afraid
lungs fisting the air amulet against . . .
you could stop reading
but the pulse in your hands has led you here

Sources

Title page

    Nor Hall, *The Moon and the Virgin,* Harper & Row, 1980.

Untying the tongue

    Nicole Brossard, *These Our Mothers,* Coach House Quebec Translations, 1983.

    Erich Neumann, 'Narcissism, Normal Self-Formation and the Primary Relation to the Mother', *Spring* (1966).

    Victor White, *Soul and Psyche: An Enquiry Into the Relationship of Psychotherapy and Religion,* Collins, 1960.

    Hélène Cixous, 'The Laugh of the Medusa', *New French Feminisms,* Schocken Books, 1981.

    Daphne Marlatt, 'Musing with Mothertongue', *Tessera* (*Room of One's Own,* 8:4, 1984).

Induction

    Hélène Cixous, 'The Laugh of the Medusa.'

Up from under

    H.D., *Thought and Vision,* City Lights Books, 1982.

    Nor Hall, *The Moon and the Virgin.*

Crafts(man)ship

    Annie Leclerc, *Parole de femme,* Grasset, 1974.

III

DAPHNE MARLATT AND BETSY WARLAND

DOUBLE NEGATIVE

For Nicole Brossard and Jane Rule

1

DOUBLE NEGATIVE

rereading reverses to resist   resists to reverse the
movement along the curve of return   as the well turned
phrase turns on herself to retrace her steps   reorient
and continue in a difference voice

LOLA LEMIRE TOSTEVIN

29/5/86 16:13
past Sydney

'Ladies and Gentlemen, could I
 have your attention please?'

4:13 past Parramatta
beyond Vancouver and the
Pacific

travelling backwards through the
actual, Sydney to Perth, it's
actually end of November down under
early summer in our veins
May white and pink studding our
northern expectation

                         not studding no
                         it does not *stand*
                         our desire
                         moves continuous around
                         surround, this is no
                         horse stable

'bring your meal tickets and place them
on your table for inspection by the
head waiter'

sun haze blinds our faces facing east
'travelling backwards through Australia'
you said through
                    (not across
                    not over

we chose to be in
these brick suburbs
moving into gum, among
fat-lettered graffiti

          DRIVE
          DRIVEL
                    under
                    pigeon cloud

we chose this
steel line
heading into Blue
Mountains white
explorers took years
getting through

as if this line
shadows that across a
Canadian map except
palm trees stud this route
gum trees, kangaroo

this is not description this
power of the other
(half of the world
                spelled out

i say *them* to *you*

kangaroo, lorrikeet, cockatoo
stolen words graffitied on our
northern minds
seeing sun shine in
FLOOD SIGN

          revelling in it

17:00
Katoomba

i recognize
these sandstone cliffs eucalyptus blue sky
outline of rose
lower lip kiss of night
(upper half a world away
tree ferns whirling coal smoke low over rooftops

we entered this
         here
Robyn threading us deep
into blue bush aboriginal sacred look / outs
creviced waterfalls
our bodies these Blue Mountains
mesmerized by gum tree glisten bird calls echoing
across self-possessed valleys

it could have been any century
it could have been before our counting

now we walk down dining car aisle
tables set for dinner
cutlery chiming
         in the sway
table cloths folded
         over edges of settings

like you and me
        in Robyn's bed
        high ceiling
        cold room dawn
        birds chaotic din of sound
              ka   toom   ba
                            ba
                  toom
              ka
           toom toom
                ka
           ka ka ka
          toom
            ba
              ba ka ba ka ba ka
          toom
            ba
              toom toom
              toom toom
         kaka
            toom
                   ba

night falls fast
through glass these blue notes run
                    (ka   toom   ba)
till your reflection develops
legs stretched out my eyes there too
your hand moving across the page

point of view
night turns the lens around

and though eucalyptus scents the air
we smell only its memory
                        (ka

                    toom
                                        ba)

pouring the ten year Pinot Noir
'you have the first sip, lovey'
                        'umm' smile clap of hands
you alight delight

travelling backwards through Australia
rim of glass on our lips

30/5 8:50
past Menindee

passed at night through
Nellungaloo, Derriwong, Micabil
dense mallee scrub
saltbush, belah, rose wood scrub
rock words tumbling dream
rocked sheep / sleep
rolled in our bunks
me above you below
in our ANR plaid blankets, no
rolled in the original glow our bodies
in the one berth sun and train smell on our
skin, soft, red earth soft
mounds of breast, belly
radiant in the womb-

                holding

motion of this
train

       traine, to
       feminize (part of
       a(d)dress)
            and not merely in tow

       you, you who know

we go inside

       out

into the womb of the continent
ochre, red earth, salt plain

evening the pink
rim of the dark the Darling
cuts an artery through, we stare in the
light, looking for kangaroo
bouncers, both
feet on the ground

prim paws, perked ears, they pound
the rim of the real their territory
we their dream roar through

staring, 'i don't believe it'
we who are gone
into the realm of the disappeared
        un/
                original here
minus the smell of earth, the glisten
of mudhole in the light, the ground
eye view of bilby, ant
thirst, dust
a dream
        we no longer remember
dingo talk didgeridoo style
(mimicked at Central Quay by a street hawker
performing 'the real thing' for the kids
who do perhaps remember

'from the beginning'
ab / original

we use their words for things, places
and they are different in our mouths

the oldest living language group in the world

we don't know where they came from
we can't go back
not to the roots we know

Indo-European words, dead wood
sentences tracking
across the untracked, the
intractably here

13:05
Mannahill

none of either

saltbush, mallee, mulga dotting earth's red skin
'scrub' and 'plain'
scrubbed clean from plain as day she's just a plain Jane
who lives here
stares back unseen from windows we flash past
in constant motion lulled by the movement carrying us
forward into ourselves
we are fed we sleep are held nameless and content
umbilical track leading us to names on a map
Yunta, Paratoo, Ucolta, Yongala
words we head for down this birthing canal
'the oldest living language' shaping our tongues lips
to speak it out (though we do not know the meanings)

magnetic field of sounds
mouths move in anOther motion

14:50
Peterborough

we carry it with us
manna a kind of dew
falling from heaven as water does

as yours do

        you remember Katoomba's 'falling waters'
        'the falling together of many streams'
        freshness spraying our faces as we
        nosed in behind its
        grass-tree, banksia, fern

        you said they were us, the mountains

unimaginable here though here changes
in a sentence glancing off Peterborough
wheat fields – this?
dry stubble glistening afternoon sheep

wool gathering, light thoughts
scatter as we clack by
    (we are
        (them

stubble legs on the table in the sun

indulgences (Schweppes soda water in its
black and gold can
        (royal palms in a backyard
        Jamestown now, after the Governor

the royal we
glancing off, gazing out

but we are not
apart from it
's incessant stream
the landscape pours through

us filled with it, held and
rocked backward, content or not
kinetic at all points in touch
with coming incessantly
into
            THIS, this

image cattle climb the
soft mound of hill lost
dip or cleft a
V to view

                                'this little entry'

                                'mine take forever'

take forever
crossed then by

a cloud, rose-breasted

this the imaginary
we enter

17:00
coming into Port Pirie

prickly pears rimming wheat fields
palm trees grain elevators
signs mutating like mixed metaphors
Peterborough, Jamestown, Gladstone, Port Pirie
anglo overlays in the name of
see-vill(ain)-I-say-tion
stiff upper lip a thin line noosing the coast of
(ab) original country

sun heading down cord leads us forward
now turned around we head for outback
Woomera 'prohibited area. . . weapons testing range'
bordering the largest aboriginal 'occupied lands'

PROhibit (whose CONscience)
PRO inhabit (whose CONtrol)
whose weapons
whose land
let's face it
the PROS (he's a real. . .) are the CONS (what a . . .)
and if language could
it would flash TILT TILT   GAME OVER
co(i)ns CONS
PROS & CONS

PRO: 'before, in front of, according to'
(Adam before. . . the Gospel according to. . .)

                                                               &

                                         CONS: 'conjunx,
                                               wife'

women as CONS: 'contrā, against, opposite'
                                       to
                                       PROS

that is
behind, after, without a version

negative feminine space

walking into the diner
'are you ladies alone'
                                'no'
                                       'we're together'

i look out the window
déjà vu:
        nothing looking at nothing

two women outback
down under
add it up – two negatives make a positive

i wonder about the physics of language
as we rim Spencer Gulf
                   tide out

stray colours of set sun held in tidal pools
                              the horizon a galah

we sip ten years as our pupils dilate
four eclipsed suns in the rising dark
the V-U be/coming our REFLECTION: 'to bend back'
convex con-cave we sit in
twenty-four hours from
                    Ka

                    toom

                              ba
you send me kisses from the end of the seat
on the map Bookaloo, Woocalla, Wirrappa
names that twitter like small birds
in the scrub we aim for

off the map
opening up the Subject
hands a manual alphabet

                    i sign your V

                    PROHIBITED AREA

    CONS: French, cunts

    the imaginary

                    two women in a birth

88

31/5 8:45
Deakin

'watching nothing going by'

woke up to desert, the Nullarbor
(nul arbor) saltbush tall, nothing bigger
than a boulder

        there's nothing there, they said
        its beautiful, they said

red earth, red-dust stained brush
grey salt bush, black railroad ties
blue (eye-blue) sky
        this translation of colour into
black on white
reading left to right as red comes in
right to left in my left eye

we pass through settlements with English names
Cook, Denman, Hughes, houses cling
to the artery the 'Long Straight' is

        through 'nothing' 'no one'
        inhabits only marks
        the cairns the
        abandoned cars

visual evidence of someone's
passing through
      (not here
            we are swallowed up
            as i birth you in /
            to the transitory
                 coming full
                         speed/time:
                         the relation to
                         there

                                 no berth here
                                 we are in space (red, red
                               your flesh i taste
                               fully distended
                               transiting no place
                               eyes dark our
                               skin intact we
                               travel *this*
                               here
                                    (saltbush

far as the eye can see

what it can't
the caves that under
lie our day – Koonalda, Weebubbie
their black lakes, their blowholes
deep as our own
something kept us awake

as we went through Ooldea
'the only natural water flow on the Nullarbor'
a subterranean river surfacing where
the Irish woman, Daisy Bates
lived out her life as Kabbarli (grand
mother
        choosing this place
of 'very thin soil cover'
this people who know how to
live with the
'deathless body'

'Welcome to Western Australia' the sign said

the desert on either side
identical

10:33
Forrest

'sometimes, you know,
when you see a scrub tree on the horizon,
it looks like a camel coming across the desert'

there are wild camels
but we've not seen them

imagin-a-nation in the heart of
                              'nothing'
when not / thing comes unhinged
                              far as the eye can see

there are birds, insects, mammals, reptiles, scrub trees,
bushes, grasses
thriving outside The Gaze
(can we see what we do not value)

red ocher over
red ocher dry-sea train
frame after frame
of red ochre menstrual stain
(source of earth's life blood)
over and ochre
even the horizon
unable to dam her flowing sand

over and ochre

'its calming, not boring'

this morning 7 am at Cook
twenty minutes out in it the air so thin   sweet
our presence minimal
you elated, your i in the camera
sunrise shine on rails   heaven in your eyes

we move in a straight trajectory after Ooldea
the 'longest stretch of straight railway in the world'
a line of thought 478 kms long
studded with former Prime Ministers
who knew how to put their names on the map

Watson, Fisher, Cook, Hughes, Deakin, Reid
settlements of identical houses facing the track
each with fire extinguisher by front door
occasional human figures stare motionless
this symmetry focusing the i to test screen patterns

time exposure

rock bottom sea bed we lie in
you pulled me under last night
sucking me out through my womb   inside out
re-versed writing across bed into sky
touching holding everything
words my only boundary
the desert on either side of my mind

13:35
Rawlinna

waiting for another train to pass
you pace the car, interrogate the conductor
'isn't there any way to get out?'
sun beckoning hot through air
conditioned glass

('seeing is believing'
not walking out in it

he says we got to
stay on track, go on

leaving our mark
shit and toilet paper
shredded at high speed
so nothing's left

nul and nothing
come up often
passing

by
/e as in

passing on. . .

from whose I-V-U?
red dust rufous kangaroo
getting slowly up
sleep disturbed

serene the
emu train stalks
eyeing us

the dream they are
we are

        full of them
        their power
        that of the momentary
        we dream into
        synchrony

        touching you
        i touch kangaroo
        lick my way through
        your red fur

        the emu walk my lips do
        at your blowhole
        breathing stars, moon
        saltbush scrub

15:25
Zanthus

trees now startling
gum's bark washed in red sun slant
re mind
of arbutus ardor of our home leaning out to sea but we
near 'highest point of the Trans-Australian Railway –
404 m above sea level'
                        then it's down to breaking waters
Indian Ocean at dawn
your Mound of V pulling me
o contraction Star of V-us
first letter of another alphabet
                        lit language we star(e) at

we will open the bed and chant our stars down
into the sway of unuttered texts
                        (make a wish)
as the matter of language reinvents itself all over again

yet now stopped in our tracks
null
an odd
stillness
addiction to movement i'm restless irritable
still want to get out
pressed like flora under glass

the map says myall, bulloak, spinifex, mallee, salt and blue
bush, salmon gums
ride of wave
we wait for the freight to pass
its rush
i had wanted to be less descriptive
be as the Nullarbor 'not any tree'
no syntax only syllables
no train of thought

yet the urge is to gather as a wave to the sea
handwriting waving as eye passes through
like all those children on backyard fences
sentences as waves
o contractions ('she didn't say nothing')
of double negatives
TRAIN: 'tragh-, contracts'
o contractions
from a small room
the shutter opening and closing

20:02
Kalgoorlie

when we get out and walk
ground rises to meet our feet
in unexpected ways
                        sea legs / rail
legs in Kalgoorlie

      'found any gold
      on the streets?' he says

the old clichés
travellers greet travellers with

      (i rail, eye rail

and the young girls in town
stand on the corner
exhibiting theirs

        (rails involve
        ends eventually

                  'the breaks'
                  and how to make them

no prison this
inert train half-

empty now seems
faded

movement is its life
anticipation
we perpetuate
in the barcar
filled with a tawdry
waiting

stopped we are not
        sleep walking
                through history
                evident here as ornate
                balconies, mine head, old
                disaster clippings

                'the real Kalgoorlie'

                merely remains

we are waiting to enter, re-enter
the rhythm again
of instant
        (by instant

                being
                about to be, this

imperceptible shift
      we will slip away (like)
ground rolling out from under

      the gradual
      thunder of coming
      in our ears

we will do
the walk the emus do
the me / you train that doubles us
into the not:

           here

the words and what
they tow along

1/6 5:45
Number 2 Cut
'Is 29 m deep. . . Known as Explosion Hill'

knock knock 'Good Morning'
cuppas at out door
rolling of bed
                (slept like a baby)
roll up the blind pitch black out there
us pitching forward
                   'all empty cups please'
he rattles down the hall
'i haven't even finished'
soon at the end of the line he wants to go home
period

packing it up
packing it in
rose on horizon rim
down to the sea i saw nothing
frantic search for lost contact on bathroom floor
                       (losing contact)
and now
          you unzip unfold hang up
in a room three times as large
and suddenly we feel cramped
in someone else's house

where are we

twelve miles from the sea
in a flesh coloured room
one rose petal on the floor
still

and the memory of your hot-soft flesh
unfurled last night in the sway in the rattle
and the wheels rolling under

o grand spread of the Moreton Bay Fig

now jumpy out of con/text
no body of movement holding us
'Number 2 Cut'
the cord severed from us both
we had not wanted it to end

heads out the door
i/s squint
the frame enlarged to sun and 360 degrees
language as billboards
feet unsteady
where to focus
life in 3-D
everything an inter/ruption

then a gradual sensation
of the Great Wheel rolling under us
of the Great Womb we call earth
not solid not still
but an ever turning threshold
its movement carrying us into
THIS:

   'what is about to be said'

        here

2

CROSSING LOOP

One dives quite naturally *into reality as if it were a valid category, an adequate landscape. . .*

NICOLE BROSSARD

B. There were things we left out, for instance our encounters with people on the train. Those people we were seated with for meals who were really an interruption in our sensual, mesmerized experience of moving through the land.

D. Well, we were so absorbed in being present to it [almost as if we were being born again in this very encapsuled and intimate experience, two in a berth/birth/byrth to bear in a certain direction, forwards say –].

B. I was aware of the different choices people make on a train. For instance, those who would leave their door open a lot and would want to watch people walking by and be seen in return. People who went to the lounge car and played games with each other for hours on end and were really into encountering strangers, making friends, making a community on the train.

D. We'd decided not to fly so that we could be *in* the landscape so of course we didn't want to be distracted by human encounters.

B. Exactly! [the human body as distraction, bodies as magicians making everything else disappear like billboards overlaying landscape, our bodies their envy of others' attention, how we prevent each other from being present to other forms of life].

D. We also didn't admit any of the tradition of how trains have been depicted, we didn't contrast how we were experiencing the train, from the inside, with how it's so often imaged from the outside as this powerful industrial monster whose rhythms and approach are seen as very much like the male orgasm – how it used to be imaged as steaming towards you down the track, or even towards the waiting female tied to the rails, which gets pretty obvious! We didn't refer to any of that. We talked about coming but made it female coming and the cyclical nature of female orgasm is really different from the one-track crescendo of male orgasm. What we really didn't deal with is how when you're on a train you are on the one track. It's not cyclical. But that was part of the tension of talking about the landscape which surrounds you as you're going through it, and the rails which lead only in one direction forward to your destination.

B. It wasn't that way for me because i saw the tracks as the umbilical cord, the track as representing our continuous dependency on the earth which we're never really cut free from. Also, the train is constantly starting and stopping, departing and arriving, coming and waiting at crossing loops and in that sense it's cyclical [as rhythm is cycling back repeating itself, the rhythm of our movement everything].

D. I suppose what we wanted to continue was this being held in the rocking motion of the train which is very womblike [when you're inside it you don't see where you're going and the train rocks from side to side, a body

108

that's carrying you so all you can do is let yourself be carried, passive voice. but we are *active* in our desire and part of what we desired was to be out in the desert as an image for a certain way of being. what we were passing through was the real subject of our writing, not the train].

B. Why do you think we didn't write about what we left out on the surface of the poem? [the body the editor *extrême,* the brain selecting only 5-10 percent of the stimulus of any given moment].

D. We were caught up in the narrative fictional frame of heading down that track, even if we translated *to* somewhere as *through* somewhere. And we were so into rewriting the train experience from a female perspective that we didn't want to admit any of the imagery from the tradition because it would have contaminated our alternative version [vision].

B. Well, we certainly talked about the mainstream literary tradition but to write about it would have taken us outside of ourselves and what was happening [yes the trace is there on the brain but we colour outside the lines referentiality's locus shifted]. It was in the process of rewriting that i became aware of a different tradition. Part of the time in Australia we were at a couple of conferences with Nicole (Brossard) who was fascinated by the desert and was writing about it in her new novel. After we returned to the coast and had begun revisions i began to think about Jane's (Rule) first book which is set in the desert. Thinking about their work i began to have a sense that there is some kind of a North American lesbian tradition of exploring the feminine in relation to the desert which is usually seen as an arena for *male* activities. I find it quite exciting that there's this female movement into the desert saying 'this is mine too and i relate to it in a different way.'

D. So we want to get off the train, get off the narrative track, and move out into the desert in a different way?

3

REAL 2

In Pitjantjara and, I suspect, all other Aboriginal languages there is no word for 'exist', everything is in interaction with everything else. You cannot say, this is a rock. You can only say, there sits, leans, stands, falls over, lies down, a rock.

ROBYN DAVIDSON

Travelling backwards through Australia

our seat backwards i had wanted one facing forwards am disappointed you say 'it's more relaxing this way' i joke' it should be familiar – it's how i was born' breech backwards back / words behind my back unable to see what lies ahead (lies are ahead) spine an antenna for wordless sightless first perception back spine / book spine no title pages blank we wait for / words travelling backwards through the factual annotated 'Strip Map' of natural (Mother) & His / torical references distances and their lineal names we move through not along not across not over like so many millions of women who passed through then 'passed away' their f. (actual life stories succinct in chiseled head/stones (at best) forever through with the ties that bind our faces facing east we choose this *through* this 'In one side and out the opposite' this 'Among or between; in the midst of' this 'By the means' this 'Here and there in' this 'From the beginning to the end' this 'Finished with' this 'Without stopping for' this 'Because of ' this 'Out in the open. . . in every part' what is woman (on a train)?

'We entered this'

as if (blue note) water doesn't sing (ka . tomb . ah) an air
of the under wells up purely from hydrostatic pressure. o
the permeable stratum you sank well into. this is what the
women know sunk in upholstered couches opening their
doors and closing them creates a threshold children cross.
this under. this world the private. into. one another. your
ka crosses mine to all intents and purposes invisible. intent
in the shadow a closed door creates a stone rolled over the
mouth. the mouth groans sings its fervid blue note. 'you
you' muffled under the weight of the others the ones who
do not sing out loud. and the children coming for some-
thing peer into other worlds as the doors open and close on
private places. in transit publicly across the Great Dividing
Range that places most of this continent in a rain shadow.
this shared weather does not mean the mixed grey of our
coast monumental thighs breasts slide into (islands touch-
ing under the water). this is the brilliance of rainless
weather everyone discrete a brilliance flesh dryly supports.
but they are opening doors and when they glance up water
artesian wells in their eyes.

The rim of the real their territory

the 'roos' stare back sometimes retreat bouncing away
from the claim of our gaze ricochet off our invading reality
tail's forceful push on red earth like our eyes evade glance
off city sidewalks ('think I'll get me some tail') or in the
night licking dew off the road mesmerized by headlights
farmers with their 'roo bars' protection from the impact of
colliding realities steel fist drives on which reel are you in
the 'abos' stare back sometimes retreat their gaze not
noosed by written language (that's what you say) or is it
Dreamtime a vision we can only imagine in theories like
collective memory whatever it is they see differently until
them i had not known the power of a culture shapes the
substance of our eyes makes us citizens on a cellular level
yet there are aberrations mute mutations whose ocular
language goes largely undetected by the linguistic mass the
muscles between the eyes & tongue straining to translate
stutter bewildering syntax synapse of alternate routes
while He insists on 'chicks' 'roos' 'abos' ('only nicknames,
mate') sells His picture collage postcards of Australia's
exotic animals: emu, kangaroo & Aboriginal in the desert
in the margin the 'wild zone' losing the proper train of
thought off the track the kanyala stare back and we see
ourselves not reflected but re/called out of this Kangaroo
Court re /called out of the Fathers' optical illusions
changing the reel inside out into the womb of the conti-
nent ochre, red earth, salt plain the wheels turning below

us the factual wheels of our knowing that move us for
words to the rim of our writing from the centre of our
speaking the intractably here what is woman (in the
desert)?

Stares back unseen

to lift some words (off the page) pick them up and run with them (here) to cite to quote is to move into fiction as if it isn't here she stares back *unseen* sighted / sited. 'the man's job at least takes him out of that square kiln of a dwelling. . .' seeing out of what we haven't or as glimpses (dreams) his wife is in the moving window frame extinguishing a fire her thirst to see a different actual – fiction cited here in light of what she lives:

'stuck day after day, week after week, in the square metal box, with a brood made fractious by heat.' Jane or Joan or Janet several variations under one roof (galvanized tin). in that cinematic light it's her hands on the table raised in an o amazing what's she brought in now? not another joey lifted from dead kanga's pocket on the highway. 'we were always bringing them home and most of them died, poor things.' the actual she's remembering, actually Janet not some dictionary entry.

it's not words / it's in words moved by the very sound of mallee leaves angled downward from the sun (a droop even the stoop describes) red earth fragrance of the very dry the salt (bush) the fire scarred (seeds that will only germinate then) all fiction to the unexposed what is accessed: the X posed, situated so as to mark the spot and not unrelated to us. setting bread on the table it's plain

117

Jane we've been here before making a home in the desert
dreaming more than survival dreaming domestic paradise
in the heart of the lost. as if there could be some arrange-
ment with/in the unarranged the deranged the out on the
range (kangaroo killing for sport). as if, as *if* (wishes were
camels and we could ride) off into our own making.

Light thoughts

shudder of the train heading for the heart CAMERA: 'room'
in your hands my shutter opening and closing X posing
negatives in the womb obscura night i/s focus through
anOther window-lens camera within camera womb within
room we 'PHOTO, light + -GRAPH, to write' the FILM: 'pel-,
skin' our bodies (all ova carry X chromosomes) Tri-X 'light
sensitive' Jane writing of Evelyn first seeing the desert as
'empty' (negative space) how can this barrenness teem with
life how can this once have been sea bottom – the desert
unbelievable, dangerous (what is woman?) but we are not
apart from it Jane's protagonist seeing that 'The earth's
given out. Men can't get a living from it. They have to get
it from each other.' the desert a different economy (her
own woman?) yet there's uranium to be mined, sacred
aboriginal sites to plunder Ann seeing 'beauty' yet Evelyn
doubtful (no place free from this violent taking) Jane at
the table thinking desert thinking desire the two she writes
driving out into it away from casino cathedrals to a lake of
'a blue so deep' no trees 'nothing . . . but an Indian
reservation' the alkaline water 'lovely for swimming' lake
not worth developing where women's desire X changes into
a foreign current/cy ('Men can't get a living from') desert
dune-wave currents

> but we are not
> apart from it

> 's incessant stream

'You could almost imagine there were no other people' Jane at her table typing 'lightning' 'large drops' and 'The storm bellied over them' as mine gathers around you in this room within a room this text within a text through this 'treeless plain' Jane punching out the keys what is woman (in her own fiction)?

Two women in a birth

what is there between them? in this in. desire in their desire room in their room somebody in the body of not in but in the doubling of. mise en abyme. out in the outback we are in the desert then or the abandoned. *the desert of ice of love of stolen dreams desert of the heart.* but what if the boundary goes walking? refuses to be that place the hero enters with his *gold* his *drums* his *caravans* – o *the desert generals the desert fathers the desert rats the desert revolution.* (we saw hoofprints of camels and never camels but scrub and many varieties of: we stood in the middle of nothing and it was full.) bleak obstacle-boundary-space to and for his adventures ground to his figure and exploits grave-cave she has rolled over in all that red dust (the year is endless here) given herself a shake and birthed into subject. the inconceivable doubling herself into life no slouch-backed beast (even double humped) heading for Bethlehem but the doubling of 'woman' into hundreds camped in the middle of desert outside Pine Gap's nuclear base, and the voice of the desert is the sound of their singing out their anger relentless and slow as dunes walking. we are off the train in order to be in the desert no longer the object of exchange but she-and-she-who-is-singing (as the women have always sung) this body *my (d)welling place,* unearthed.

There's nothing there

dense fog out window Canada geese honk in flying V
your mound of V its exquisite V-U ('V ancestral to the
letter U') i imagine U (her hand pulled to 'The U-rune...
the mother of manifestation') and this V of geese, the fog
thick and me alone V indicating 'velocity, verb, verse,
version, verso, versus, victory, volt, vowel' o blowholes o
lightning o coming full speed / time: the relation to there,
there-there – there's nothing there (comforting of our
childhood fears) flying V sign for peace the marches the
Vision the burning of draft cards ban the bomb earth
mothers free love flowers slipped into barrel ends of riot
control rifles rejection of one authoritative version verso
turning over a new leaf women's lib black power versus the
Great White Fathers' Vietnam their armies undisciplined
riddled with deserters DESERT: 'dēserere, to abandon' drug
haze boomerang of the Fathers' arrogance (every cloud has
a silver lining) their solace the desert, receptacle of seminal
explosions Virility shooting sky high environmentalists'
protest, there's nothing there – the Fathers' retort – it's
just a bunch of sand/box these boy-men play in who will
inherit their just deserts the desert site of His testing the
desert site of Her texting (nothing looking at nothing) this
is not the Mirror Stage but a glimpse of her own ecosystem
of emptiness 'If your mind is empty, it is always ready for
anything' her mind a womb its blood the 'watching
nothing going by' embrace of the churinga (the 'deathless

body') this texting the abandoned made new in her 'In the beginner's mind there are many possibilities; in the expert's mind there are few' what is woman (in her emptiness)?

Imagin-a-nation in the heart of

as the heart surrounded by all this flesh feels its weight (the pressure of pumping blood through such a system) throws up its hands in surrender the heart is never isolate never away (women cannot get away) as the people who inhabit this emptiness will tell you heartland laid waste (desert is not waste) dug up for uranium irradiated in nuclear testing (the fragile ecosystem the heart is) will fence off sacred sites to keep out the acquisitive the heart is consumed the heart is not allowed to throb for pleasure in what surrounds it (imagine a nation at home in the 'deathless body') the heart must be used (up) (imagine a nation uncommitted to surplus profit) working for love not pay imagination is at home with emptiness imagination a-muses herself with the emptiness of words and boards the train of the sentence empty handed and makes off with it de-riding the end point of the Final Product (she is not for termination after all) she is well on her way to de-railing the 'long straight' which can only see its own track while she is out on either side (surrounded she knows does not mean surrender) she is also she is desert come in waves the waves she rides she rises up and overflows the words a round around the word *surround*

He says we got to stay on track

well trained he is we are the only difference being it's his job
he profits from it stopped for twenty minutes desert
beckoning through conditioned glass he doesn't make the
rules–just enforces them dissociative division of labour no
one directly responsible for anything fill out a form some-
one will get back to you form letter replying to form (form
is form) she looks out the window what she longs for is the
absence of the symbolic to lose track of disappear into this
emptiness (his key ring tight around her neck) why this
vigilance it's not survival of the fittest (he no dingo she no
emu) hand to mouth not their relationship no their hunt
is on another plain food for thought word to word fight for
defining whose symbolic dominates whose (Adam com-
plex) she wants to migrate she wants to mutate she wants
to have no natural predators be nothing looking at nothing
thrive in her own absence be out of focus out of range of
The Gaze hide out from The Law under assumed names
but there's no way out even the desert cannot escape
imagin-a-nation of the imaginations of the 113 billion who
have lived and recorded their mindscapes (real to reel) she
reads the 'Percentage of those whose memory survives in
books and manuscripts, on monuments, or in public
records: 6" she calculates possibly 1 percent represents her
gender's memory wonders how woman has even survived
the wedge-tailed eagle circles above and the train begins to
roll as her hand moves across the page spiral movement

(imagin-a-nation) here she can rest here she can play encounter her anima(l) self pre-sign pre-time touching you i touch kangaroo words forming then shifting desert dunes her desire to untrain herself undermine every prop(er) deafinition she throws the switch on train as phallus ('bound for glory') train as salvation leaves it behind at the crossing loop feels words falling from her like the 50 million skin scales we shed each day breathing stars, moon saltbush scrub your hand moves across my body (imagin-a-nation) and we settle into this endless motion once again settle into the beginninglessness the endlessness of this page this desert this train this shared desire wholly here with a passion that humbles us what is woman (in her own symbolic)?

No train of thought

for Robyn Davidson

yet we are back on it with the sentence (s)training toward
completion finale as if this as if here were the endpoint
culmination as a wave does not waveraves to begin again
the falt er the fallo(w)ver is the followthrough she walked
on over 'sandhills for ever, they all looked the same. . .
What if there's no water, what will I do? . . . Just keep
walking. Just one step at a time. . .' as if one were only nul
numb over and out swimming with her camels through
the heat toward some destination which is when it will be
over finis end stop swimming through the waterless the
seabed risen ages old through the deathless through the
rolypoly (salt work) her project (the sentence) is to get to
the end of the rail of the bed and we are sleepers laid under
(one by one) by the track saying this is it this is rock
(bottom) line yet 'the self in a desert becomes more and
more like the desert' (s)and word wavering sense bounda-
ries 'stretched out for ever' and when she stops and when
she rises mind 'rinsed clean' this is no longer rock, this-
and, this unapart from this wave part of a sea that wavers
falls forward gathers 'This, which everything acts upon,
acts'

Of instant (by instant

standing on the bed sleepers side by side rails blanketing
we their dream overhead standing on the bed (point of
view) rails meet on the horizon ∧ form a giant caret
from 'there is lacking' from 'kes-, castrate, caste, incest'
The story of ^{Wo}∧Man standing in our room looking
down at my mound invert(ed) ∧ lines bend toward
one another meet at point where eyesight fails point of
desire always moving ahead of us do parallel lines actually
meet – in light years perhaps yet it's *what* we see this illu-
sion the eye momentarily believing in unity (believing *is*
desire) seeing is. . . we believe ourselves into ecstasy: 'to
displace, drive out of one's senses'

point

of   v-u

Jane at her table (in the desert) u at your table (in the
desert) Nicole at her table (in the desert) and me at this
table (in the desert) not there but there writing the not
here inverts turning perspective upside down writing
morphogenetic lines which refuse to be read parallel
writing desert lines (mirage between the eyes) writing rail
lines (illusion our desires meeting) lines that carry us off
pull us over earth's edge / end, table the sea we might fall
off its Other the desert (fear of its never ending) reassur-
ance of the page's turning Barthes maintaining narrativity
not possible without Law and History (immaculate
conception no parthenogenesis) caret caret u of the not

here steel yourselves rail at His One Essential Story telling and retailing of male quest escape from the metaphorical womb and the conquering of it *this* is where the v inverts reveals how u and me and he are all held fast by the wombworld we are ever dependant on Robyn in the Gibson Desert finally *present* (theshold to dreaming, creation, spiritual vision) 'I too became lost in the net and the boundaries of myself stretched out for ever' where all points of view converge where eyes close signalling bodies to trust the turning as we float off the page held tender & fierce in our terrifying difference what is woman (in her ecstasy)?

We had not wanted it to end

wanting not to get there but getting there pleasure goes
around in circles evades the end point heads backward into
the unknown (o birth) the peeling back wide-eyed feeling
a way through flood tides well up (highest tides of the
century) shifting ground face down not on ANR plaid
blankets no but grass rock that rocks with the motion of
what has carried us strident cries rosella flash of wings into
Perth skies this everturning threshold no line is nothing to
cross or resist your mouth mine mouths us in suspense the
evercoming trembles on. . .

reading us in what is out of place out / standing out of that
which (normally) is we are arctic we are summer tasting a
water not so salt as marked by it forever lingual tongue in
alkaline caves succeeds accedes to the pre (prairie free)
symbolic flowers here a desert's standing sea the ocean in
us throbs to meet

we bilingual reading rock reading sand word reading us in

IV

DAPHNE MARLATT AND BETSY WARLAND

READING AND WRITING BETWEEN THE LINES

Collaboration is a specious term for the writing you and i do together. . . and here, even here, hovering between third person and second person pronoun, to choose second with its intimacy seems to me indicative of how i write with and to you. you my co-writer and co-reader, the one up close i address as you and you others i cannot foresee but imagine 'you' reading in for. and then there's the you in me, the you's you address in me, writing too. not the same so much as reciprocal, moving back and forth between our sameness and differences.

in our doubleness, no, our plurality as we read (for) and write (to) you, all the you's in each other reading and writing too – a polylogue, such bends and twists – you see how this writing rivers out to various mouths immediately?

which is why i find it difficult to use the word collaboration with its military censure, its damning in the patriot's eyes (the Father appears here with his defining gaze, his language of the law). collaboration implies that who we are collaborating with holds all the power. the lines are drawn. but perhaps it's the very subversion implicit in collaboration that i might see in our favour were we to move between the lines. when i see us as working together reciprocally, then what i see us working at is this subversion of the definitive. running on together (how I love prose), reciprocal in this, that the holes we make in such a definite body leak meaning we splash each other with, not so much working as playing in all this super-fluity, wetting ourselves with delight even, whetting our tongues, a mutual stimulation we aid and abet (entice) in each other.

Let me slip

'let me slip into something more comfortable'

         she glides across the
room
lābi, to glide, to slip

(labile; lābilis
labia; labialis)
     la la la
'my labyl mynde. . .'
lābilis, labour, belabour, collaborate, elaborate

'The Hebrews named their letters, some guttural. . .
others dental. . . and so they call others, labial, that
is letter of the lips'

slip of the tongue
      'the lability of innocence'
labium 'any of the four folds of tissues of the female
external genitalia'
four corners of the earth
four gates of Eden
      labia majora (the 'greater lips')
      la la la
        and
       labia minora
      (the 'lesser lips')

not two mouths but three!
slipping one over on polarity

             slippage in the text
you & me *collābi, (to slip together)*
in labialization!
slip(ing)page(es)
like notes in class

o labilism o letter of the lips
o *grafting* of our slips

labile lovers
'prone to undergo displacement in position or change in
nature, form, chemical composition: unstable'

giving the one authoritative version the slip
graft, graphium, graphein, to write

                slippery lines

thought is collaboration

Or thought is

or thought is reading one another's min(e)ds, stumbling
onto unexpected gaps, holes, wait, explosive devices – this
is not enemy territory we're speaking of or in, though each
entry can be for the other a dark side of the moon, its
sudden craters, its dry seas or season. . .

mooning (we wander aimlessly) or spooning (with a lure,
but whose?) slippery words this slippery body we tongue
between us comes between us in the ways a word can
sound 'slippage' you said
          slipping in the age it takes the mind
                    to turn around its mooring words that bind
you gave me the slip suggesting you'd slip into something
more comfortable

negligible and large, in which we are complicit and inter-
ested together to be in this body at sea with one another in
the slippage of meaning this loss of motion forward is fear,
wait, being taken off in a different direction altoge-
ther. . .

collaboration then as power play where we breaks down
into you and i and i'm tired of defining these feints of
desire, us desiring yes this third body we go chasing after
and jealousy moves in, hey what are you really after?

so let's talk about the dark side as it rises dimly behind the lit rooms of our intentions variously engaged. let's talk about the ground rules, how i can revise me but not you though i sometimes try. how we find the mean in our understanding of what we're individually after. even if it lies in two different directions? what happens to our writing when *together* to be in a body breaks down?

Not simply

not simply a working together there are challenges back-
ings up required words we graft from each other's texts
that can't be later edited out

'where are you going with this?'
'you didn't go deep enough'

rewrites re you re me losing the rhythm instinctive steps
& turns (no box / waltz here) writing 'in the dark, i saw
you. . .' the tension necessary following & leading
s)witching unpredictably the doubt –

'you've written it all; there's nothing left for me to say'
'you gave me the slip'

the elation sparking the provoking each other beyond our
endings our meanings

'i didn't know that was in there until now'

playing with each other's logic like a dream dark side of the
moon right brain conversation the erotic zones of a word
we're both attracted to stroke *arousing* our enigmatic mé-
nage à trois one nearly always on the outside edge of two
a living on it sharpening our semantic shifts slips *yā*, for the
zeal of a language intimate *(intimāre, to put in, publish,
from intimus, inmost deepest)* we risk *jealousy* the fear of
losing our voice and the afterglow of finding we haven't

And what about

and what about the talking we do that underlies or
underlines (between the lines) what gets written on the
page (what isn't there, the dark side off the record as the
waltz winds down) – are we dancing in the dark? as if the
page were a lit room read from outside while we go on
doubling behind the scene, the you of the page i subvert in
the unwritten you i walk our streets with, night, passing
the lit rooms of story i saw 'you' of your page subvert in me
biography or writing with our lives the tension necessary
between what gets said and what gets written or left (out
in the dark with other readers-in who are also us party to
the parts we play in the game, apart and not) 'you put your
whole self in' but what is yourself, your voice? as our heads
slide through semantic shifts that are not ours as language
never is

The talking we

the talking we do that underlies the underwriting assessing the risks the mutual responsibilities of each other's *liabilities, leig-, reply* in this game of double *solitaire, sole, sel, room* two lit two dark and sometimes 'two silhouettes on the shade' the embodiment the doubling of the chance of language the cards up our sleeves power play of our idiosyncratic synapses game of chance exposing the writer's sleight of hand which tricks the reader into believing in a voice in the wilderness singularly inspired here we acknowledge that all writing is collaboration here we question the delineation between the collectivity of conversation and the individual's ownership

of the written here we affirm our spiralling dominoing wandering she-speech in the talking we do between the sheets between the lines between the writing that intertwines it's all in the cards each deck a voice distinct to its own tones its rhythms its own feel its quirky selectivity (the mind only taking in 10 % of stimulation at any given moment) the card's meaning particular to the relationship of the others the *sequence, sekw-, intrinsic* to math, music, literature making love while i'm *shuffling, possibly (but quite doubtfully) O.E. scop, poet* dealing you a double deck but card sharps are liable to whet their tongues on each other's slipperiness then call for a redeal

The card you

the card you are in this full house dancing us room to room as the music shifts – and yes, who's leading who? you and me and language makes three, no baby she, *la langue,* she'll shift the rhythm on you, bend your sense, slam you into difference while you're still stumbling over your intent, trying to keep your word/s from running away with sense. . .

to keep (y)our word. eroticizing collaboration we've moved from treason into trust. a difficult season, my co-labial writer writing me in we while we are three and you is reading away with us –

you and you (not we) in me and all of us reading, which is what we do when left holding the floor, watching you soar with the words' turning and turning their sense and sensing their turns i'm dancing with you in the dark learning to trust that sense of direction learning to read you in to where i want to go although the commotion in words the connotations you bring are different we share the floor the ground floor meaning dances on. . .

whirling out to include. . .

are you trying to avoid the auto-biographical? what is 'self' writing here? when you leave space for your readers who may not read you in the same way, the autobiographical becomes communal even communographic in its contextual and narrative (Carol Gilligan) women's way of thinking – and collaborating?

Bathroom sink

at the bathroom sink
'so, do you think the collaboration is working?'

'yes. do you?'

'yes. . . i don't know what others will think of it –'

i continue to brush my teeth thinking about the word
euphemism
eu-, good + phēmē, speech   u-feminisms
all our yous (u / s) and all the others'

the words & sayings we're taught as children
so as to avoid embarrassing adults
for u it was 'fooze'
for me 'results'
the onomatopoia the practicality
these substitutions more explicit, subjective

gift of the *ghabh-,*
cohabit

'rhythmic synchrony'
a sociolinguistic microanalyst documenting the unique
rhythmic patterns of familial conversation has found the
crescendos, pauses, stressed syllables, and cutlery punctu-
ation on plates to reveal a score which is replayed and
replayed (no matter what the narrative)

are u keeping score?

'auditory touch'

lovers not only share a rhythm
but a 'sustained mirror synchrony' of movements

yes
we do write to each other's u/s
but it is out of the blue
or in the black
depending upon the time of day
or mood

a gift is not the received
o the unruliness of our selective minds
we read each other's entries so differently

or do we always write out of black & blue:
the in-juries of our *individuality, in-, + dividuus, divisible*

u-feminisms a strategy against u-thanasia
all our u/s essential (impossible to play without a full deck)

we shuffle
cut
and play into the source of our u-phoria

when we interwrite
we call each other's u-phonies out of the dark out of the
blue out of the glare of white

V

DAPHNE MARLATT AND BETSY WARLAND

SUBJECT TO CHANGE

beginning with a toss. . .

March 4, 1991

'toss [origin obscure]'

> *pre / occupation with*
> *what precedes – its profound effect*

we agree
to precede
          each
    other

occupied by sun, the day, the time
mutually

      circling around it
                – it?

      the loon or the Queen
      keeping face or
            taking the dive below

two sides of the same coin

why then the toss?

> *to pretend*
> *there is difference? reed shine*
> *on the lake: hair shine on your*
> *wet leg*

March 4, 1991

i want to edit this after & just write freely now

you know how hard it is to edit a collaboration – you can't rewrite what you say without affecting what i say in response

*

you can't look

why?

you know how i feel about being watched

*

i have this desire to draw a line and write down everything we say

let's try it

*

what's this?
reed.
r-e-a-d?
r-e-e-d

*

[the waiting, restlessness of your clothes shifting on your body]

March 5

not that precedence is everything

we are always in response to

light on the table, these drooping
       tulips,

             open onto death

                   illuminated feathers
                   drifting
                         down

the dance of talons, hopping
wing spread
always in response to

             our hunger
               fear
               desire

hawk takes precedence, makes off
with thought
thinks only present

           (worry tingles
           elsewhere. . . the cat?
while early this morning. . .

                     your taste

position makes the difference
       hawk licker – crow licked
          dying for the
            rapture

there's an immature eagle on that tree, defeathering its catch

[chair falls over as D. gets up to see] you'd be great at bird watching!

wonder what it's got?

a bird – probably a duck, i first noticed the feathers flying

*

that's the end!

no, I don't agree

otherwise we'll say too much – that makes a nice shape right there

i don't feel finished

*

it just flew off

it hasn't got a duck, it's a crow – it's landed on that tree, it looks to me like a hawk – a red-tailed hawk, that's the one i grew up with

*

i can still smell you

*

i'm not into sex & death

but the fear is a bit like that – rapture [looking it up in the dictionary] you know they all relate – a hawk is a raptor, then there's the rapture, rapt, seized by enchantment

March 6

the lesbian writer's hands
form a procession thought em/bodies

       lead to one another
leading words leading lips

finger's 'round
pencil or mound
          penis still?
         no.
       lead to one another –

shake a lead or get it
out

    how the legs shake

              at each other's
              epicenter

       epic

in the act her story

binds woman to goddess
     with/in

         divine rupture

March 6

is that leap?

no, lead [lĕd]

oh, i thought it was leap or lead [lēd]

*

i think that's the last word – sounds a bit pathological!

March 7

breaking out, you said
muscles working together in
leading you on

>   *– more that than precedence*

a kind of birthing
womb the body's largest muscle
making room in the language

>   with the heart
>   the next

where's mind?

where's mine?

quack, quack retort of ducks nesting

>   saving our queens?
>   *face cards close to*
>   *your heart?*

struggle?
re-enactment?

we do not birth ourselves

>   *under the micro*
>   *scope insects*
>   *writhe*

in sects

>   you've left

March 7

do you want me to add another line? i've got one

do

*

you're not going to take off on 'language'?

you can do it

[repeated searching through dictionary]

*

i *don't know what the fucking queens are doing in there*

are you stuck?

*well, this poem seems to be going in two opposite directions and
i can't figure out how to re-unite them. i was really excited
about something up here and we just keep getting further away
from it*

*

what are you doing?

i'm making notes of what i was trying to get to

the cat purred, walked all over the page, lay down on it. we stroked him. he purred (silky fur) then began to bite. us too. fight. your feeling it isn't a poem – just 'blather,' and that i wasn't picking up on what you were writing. my feeling your frustration, anger, and wanting to be true to the reader and our struggle for 'mine.' beginning too late in the day part of the problem – our minds needing their own idiosyncratic directions. the quotidian's power, even on our 'day off'.

missing each other's signals. my thinking your impatience is partly due to your anger at not having time to do your **own** writing (your novel) but having to respond to other deadlines (like this one). i felt betrayed as your impatience increased. felt it as early as when i wrote 'where's mine'? why i wrote it. and then felt angry when you began writing, on another page. you left. i accuse you of wanting a 'perfect poem,' and of not wanting to make yourself vulnerable to the reader. you say it 'isn't working.' it's 'blather'.

i say it's being true to the process. i don't only want to present the reader with 'perfect poems' but also the back & forth. the struggle for mine **and** the relaxing into, moving with each other into, something more than mine. that intoxicating doubling of anticipation and revelation. i didn't only intend 'mine' as a possessive but also in the sense of mining. mining the mind throughout our whole bodies.

you say it's not poetry. i'm ok with that. don't want to feel controlled by form. 'But people will look at lines on the page and expect poetry.' i suggest we could write about this, these short lines, these unpredictable spaces – our riding the currents of one another's associative and symbolic thought. for me – that's what we're doing, and sometimes – not doing. both are equally of interest. both have the potential for meaning.

where's mind? where's mine?

                            territory – & the terror at the edges
of losing our way in the mind-direction of the other.

        we talk angrily. you accuse me of leaving the collaboration
because it isn't going the way i want it to. i accuse you of jud-
gement when you say i'm getting too theoretical.

        'where's mine'? the axe split in the poem.

        i want to follow the drift evolving through earlier entries,
words, thoughts we nudge up to in various ways. the same and
different, changing as they recur. i have a sense of something
moving into focus in & through the drift & when we approach
it i get excited, connections leap, though there's always the strain
of contiguity – how much more that is disparate can touch on
what's already there & nudge it forward?

        you want to document the struggle our wandering, our
mind-blather makes along with the flights when we soar together.
for you, resistance to flying together is as important as flying to-
gether. all part of the process – nothing insignificant. although
you still use the word 'significant' when you talk about the
actions, the body-shifts you choose to record in the margin. you say
i want to write a perfect poem. we have a different understanding
of form & process – form is more organic for you, what happens.
for me form is something we make in collaboration with the
poem, a 3rd entity which develops its own process as we continue.
for you the poem is the trace of our collaboration, the record of our
ins & outs. for me the poem is something we collaborate with. it
doesn't have to be a poem you say, just because it's in lines on the
page – form isn't holy. form is holy, in the sense that it is what gets
revealed – and what it tells us then.

        we didn't talk about this before we started. i thought we
were writing a poem together with documentary asides in the
margin. you thought we were documenting our writing together.
the question of which takes precedence – & can we agree? or do
we have to?

March 7
afterthoughts

*up till now when we've collaborated we've each had indi-
vidual control of our individual pieces so we could shape them
according to our own sense of form. it's not surprising that we
should have difficulty collaborating on such a microscopic level
– it's the first time our senses of form have collided with each
other and we've had to give up individual control.*

our forms like our fingerprints? the bodies we live in. even
more indelible in their idiosyncracies than our words?

giving each other the gears we are still engaged

March 9

timing
         & the chiming words do
lead us on
         beyond our intentions

tending inwards, vortical –

         let's give it a whirl

how to keep our centres
in each other's motion?

     mouths?

         all of them

a flight of lips

         that balance
         not top or bottom heavy
         leading somewhere?

currents aren't maps

but they **move**

         sometimes barely –

         eagle floating almost still
         in high sky
            seeing the duck
            will plummet rapidly

stillness sharpening vision

tai chi: intention behind each
movement turning circles

red

tulip's drooping head against the table
breast of House Finch
have we read

what?

?

— whether there's an object to the verb —

subject

to change

March 9

are we not writing in the margin anymore? we have up until now –

do we have to be consistent?

well, i feel intimidated about it now

i feel intimidated by you – you were writing **everything** *down*

i wasn't writing everything down

let's not do it this time

but then we need to indicate why we're not

we can add a note, besides, we might not even use it

we don't know that yet

well, let's write this down

March 11

collaboration on this micro-creative level is a meditation. it insists on our sustained presence to the page and each other. when we did break away and write our own statements, our writing kept us in close contact, pulled us back to the same meditative page once again.

this process exposed our collaboration to also be a form of mediation '. . .an intervention between two disputing parties in order to effect a peaceful settlement or compromise through the benevolent intervention of *a neutral power.*' but as lesbians and feminists, we know form and language are not neutral, and when up against the wall – they vie even more fiercely than we. there is no neutral, benevolent mediator – we must also assume this role. after fear and fight, there is our love. there is our paired flight.

March 12

first there is not we but i + i. starting off on different sides (of the same coin), tossing our idiosyncratic perceptions into the ring (sand, circle, performance space, these various animals – read birds – the smell of fear and applause). these perceptions that perform almost arbitrarily it seems (will she see what i mean?) (does it matter if it means something else to her?) meaning, the elusive bird, dies into dust only to rise again in a further line aflare with connections.

connections: (we): breathtaking, when thought leaps the gap between two idiosyncratic fields of association two lives have accumulated in their separate dialects, diverse cultural origins, private value systems, unconscious dream hordes. we still argue about the pronunciation of certain words – not the same as mis-reading **reed** *or* **lead.** *and is* **mis-***reading the word? everything entered subject to change, subject to transformation in the reader's imaginary, the reader being she, after all, who constructs meaning.*

so i fears being misread, the flagrant will (raptor) wants her field day, takes off on the wing to pursue **her** *meaning. and we desires connection, (rapt) lead away, to wider horizons of each other's making, beyond limits (that first take) taken apart and given to possibility. this does not mean death, though i fears it, fears losing her way.*

March 13

yes, i + i. i for an i and i to i. my handwritten i looking very much like a semicolon, '. . . punctuation indicating a degree of separation intermediate in value between the comma and the period.' ii – the Roman numeral for 2 or ;; a double semicolon, where the separation between the comma and the period is amplified. double ambiguity. doubled possibility.

changing the subject – our feminist project. yet, the subject is always subject to change. from one perspective, we saw an eagle and duck. from the other, we saw a red-tailed hawk and crow. the difference a hundred feet makes.

how we sleep deep in trust. one side then the other, fetal fit 'round each other like quotation marks
"   "

"   "

book-ending one another's *unconscious dream hordes.* buttressing each other's night-floating i.

the relief, delight of i being only part of (i)t all. the very real difference in this from how we are absented by the domi-nators. letting go of the notion of misreading is dependent upon our knowing the difference. 'collabōrāre, com-, to-gether + labōrāre, to work.' i abandons her introductory clause for a being between comma and illusory period. she needs their double jeopardy of discovery more than her differentiating declarations, but she knows old habits die hard.

March 15

yours reads in the shape of a sandwich (toasted), the soft intimate part in the middle 'egg shelley' actually what we had for lunch in the cafe yesterday. our day off together a gap in the text. intimate, to intimate, a movement inwards from pub-lish. though i don't know that our bodies bookend the hordes which ride on regardless:

unlimited scope for mayhem watching her body move. egg Shelley. maybe a-hem, without hemming in the fertile urge fiction is, re-reading everything. . .

dreamwork: (to work) reality.

so that the object transforms into subject and back again. ***i being part of (i)t*** *– the delight as you say, lighting up as perspective shifts, illuminating. the quicksilver way connection leaps the gap between subject and object in desire. she broke the thermometer; we are degrees of thumb and forefinger pooling of liquidities. a figure of telling,*

egg shelley actually the name in play,

yours,

March 16 & 17

a telling figure, the seduction of – she(')ll!

intimate / intimate. (p)art of each other. y – ours?
generative power of our intimacy – this too must have a life
on the page. degrees of desire – what we hold in our
fingertips! yet, not to idealize. something in between
lesbian pulp romance and politically correct silence (each
puritanical in impulse). the reader needs more. we read
these words with a double voraciousness. coming out

of our shells. the writer lesbian, the reader lesbian shell
shocked? sexing the page lesbian. in our profound plurality.

'i, yōdh, hand.' this is a gamble. (the roll of. . .) possibly a
do or die. egging one another on – sandwiches originated
so gamblers could stay at the table.

doubling the stakes at our tables of chance. 'obsession,
obsidere, to sit down before' each other's writing presence
is to risk each other's inherent chaos – for here the erotic
is endlessly born.

you/r bet

March 19

*so, letters (safe on the other side). you write downstairs on your computer. i type upstairs. we pass the pages back and forth in the kitchen. not the same as sitting at the same table, writing on the one page. we are not the same, not one, sitting side by side, **sam,** together. not is where desire enters. . .*

knotting it together, as something different (to collaborate) in a body (of work), seductive, and resistant. currents at play. combatting old habits, shifting ground where we meet, quick tongue, sweet wit, cl- : not closing it.

each the other to each in our reach together. oxymoronic no doubt, in excess. yet, yes.

About the Authors

West Coast writer Daphne Marlatt has published a number of books of poetry and/or prose, including *Steveston, How Hug a Stone, Double Negative* (co-authored with Betsy Warland), *Ana Historic, Salvage* and *Ghost Works.* She was a founding member of the feminist editorial collective and magazine, *Tessera,* and has co-edited the proceedings of two feminist conferences, *In the Feminine,* and *Telling it: Women and Language across Cultures.*

Betsy Warland's books include *A Gathering Instinct, open is broken, serpent (w)rite, Double Negative* (with Daphne Marlatt), *Proper Deafinitions* and *The Bat Had.* She co-edited *In the Feminine, Telling It: Women and Language Across Cultures,* and edited *InVersions: Writing by Dykes, Queers and Lesbians.* She has also written two plays, *The Bat Had Blue Eyes,* and *Viva.*

Printed by
Ateliers Graphiques Marc Veilleux Inc.
Cap-Saint-Ignace, Québec
in August 1994.